# Marriage customs in Shakespeare's England

*In Elizabethan times, the poor could marry where they chose. The upper classes made sure their sons and daughters married well.*

*Much Ado About Nothing* ends with a double wedding – a cheerful occasion, with music and dancing. Before the couples get married, their friends and relations are actively involved in bringing them together. Don Pedro negotiates with Leonato for Claudio to marry Hero; and practically everyone in the play conspires to bring Beatrice and Benedick together. This reflects real life among upper-class Elizabethans.

3

## Declaration of marriage

There was no set legal form for marriage in Elizabethan England. In theory, if a man and a woman declared before witnesses that they were married, they were married. There were of course some legal restrictions. You could not marry a close relative, for example. But the most important restriction, from the point of view of the number of law-cases it inspired, was 'prior contract' – one of the couple being married, or contracted to be married, to someone else.

Obviously, where a simple declaration made a legal marriage, this happened rather often. Sometimes a couple who wished to part would conveniently remember a prior contract, as a way of getting 'divorced'. Or an old flame might turn up, perhaps with an eye to some property. The better-off (like the characters in this play) solved the problem by putting everything in writing. The poor, who had no property to worry about, often did not.

## Legal cause

Another method of preventing illegal marriages was contained in the marriage service, and the 'calling of the banns' which came before it. The banns were an announcement, made three times at regular church services, that a particular couple were to marry. Anyone who knew any reason why they should not had an opportunity to speak up about it. This was repeated at the marriage service itself (and is, in the Church of England service, to this day). Claudio himself responds in the play, almost causing disaster.

If Claudio had really seen Hero exchanging love-talk with Don Pedro, he might actually have had a legal case against Hero and her family. (Since both the people he saw were others in disguise, the case might have made a few lawyers rich!) When Hero is supposedly dead, Leonato is quick to

*For the wealthy, weddings were an occasion for elaborate and costly entertainment. Music, mime and dancing accompanied this sumptuous feast. Notice the absence of cutlery. Guests ate with their fingers, washed them in finger bowls and wiped them on the napkins they kept over shoulder or arm.*

SHAKESPEARE FOR EVERYONE·

# MUCH ADO ABOUT NOTHING

By Jennifer Mulherin and Abigail Frost   *Illustrations by* George Thompson

CHERRYTREE BOOKS

## Author's note

*There is no substitute for seeing the plays of Shakespeare performed. Only then can you really understand why Shakespeare is our greatest dramatist and poet. This book simply gives you the background to the play and tells you about the story and characters. It will, I hope, encourage you to see the play.*

A Cherrytree Book

Designed and produced by
A S Publishing

First published 1993
by Cherrytree Press Ltd
327 High Street
Slough
Berkshire SL1 1TX

Reprinted 2001

Copyright this edition © Evans Brothers Ltd 2001

British Library Cataloguing in Publication Data
Mulherin, Jennifer
    Much Ado About Nothing
    1. Drama in English. Shakespeare, William, 1564-1616
    I. Title  II. Series III Frost, Abigail.
    822.3'3

ISBN 1 84234 035 2

Printed in Hong Kong through Colorcraft Ltd

# Contents

offer him another bride. Marriage, for the propertied, was often as much a matter of joining two fortunes as of romantic love.

## Wedding feasts and festivities

Though it was legally possible to marry quickly and quietly, for most people, then as now, a wedding meant a party. Even the poor could hold 'bride-ales', in a hall by the church, where a collection was taken to pay for food and drink and leave something over for the couple to start married life. The bride would walk to the church with her hair hanging loose, with a wreath of flowers or corn on her head. (In the city of London, the merchants preferred a gilded crown. Some churches owned such a crown to lend to brides.)

## Something old, nothing new

It seems odd, to modern eyes, that Hero does not have a new dress for her wedding. But fine dresses were very expensive (and took a long time to make). Instead, a bride chose a favourite dress and decorated it with all sorts of temporary finery: ribbons, laces and various favours. After the ceremony, she would remove these and throw them to her guests, who would scramble for them. The most prized of these favours was her garter: whoever got it would wear it in his hat afterwards. Other favours were 'knives' (probably scissors) and pin-cases (worn hanging from a belt). Embroidered gloves were a traditional gift from a groom to a bride. In *Much Ado About Nothing*, Claudio sends Hero a pair of scented gloves.

Another custom was strewing the ground before the wedding procession with flowers or herbs – a forerunner of modern confetti. Sometimes, instead, the ground was strewn with symbols of the groom's trade: even pieces of iron if he was a blacksmith!

# The Watch

Music was an important part of wedding customs: not only the hymns in the church, but also secular music, with the bridal procession, at the bride-ale for dancing, and sometimes, under the couple's window next morning to wake them up. Big weddings, like any other gathering in Elizabethan England, were noisy affairs. If they got too rowdy, the Watch might have to intervene.

*The bellman patrolled the streets with a staff, a lantern, a bell – and perhaps a dog. He called out the time and kept a watch for fires and thieves.*

*The poor were blamed for most of the crime, but crooks came in all guises. This gentlemanly thief picks a pocket with one hand and a lock with another.*

There was no regular police force in England before the nineteenth century. The lonely roads between the towns and villages were dangerous places, where gangs of thieves might catch unwary travellers. In towns, the local authorities (the parish, or a city corporation), would appoint officers like Dogberry and his colleagues to 'keep the peace'. Their job was to patrol the streets, and literally make sure everything was peaceful.

Besides arresting drunkards and criminals, they had to look out for fires – an ever-present danger when close-packed wooden houses were lit by candles, and call out the hours for

*Marian Frith, known as Moll Cutpurse, was a notorious thief. She dressed as a man, and had the weapons, speech and drinking habits of a hardened criminal.*

citizens who did not own clocks. In many sixteenth-century towns, they were supposed to make sure everyone was indoors by perhaps nine o'clock at night. But some Elizabethans kept late hours, and the task cannot have been easy.

### Night on the tiles

Thomas Harman, an Elizabethan country magistrate who wrote a book about criminals he had met, tells how the watch raided an inn. It was one o'clock in the morning, but customers were in the garden gambling on a noisy, rough game, and a pig was roasting on a spit at the kitchen fire. The gamblers began to fight over who had won. The officers joined in, arrested them and got ready to take them to the stocks. The inn's owners came out and spoke up for their guests, saying they were genuine travellers and would leave as soon as they had eaten.

Meanwhile, the neighbours came to complain about the noise. Finding the house empty, they stole the pig 'spit and all, with such bread and drink as also stood upon the table'. The landlady shouted at the constable when she found out, but 'he laughed in his sleeve, and commanded her to dress (cook) no more at unlawful hours for any guests.' Next morning, the thieves left the spit in the street for the owners to find.

### Sturdy beggars

Dogberry would probably have recognised this situation. Petty crimes, drunkenness, gambling and arguments between neighbours would have been his main concerns, along with moving on 'sturdy beggars'. Under the Elizabethan Poor Laws, the parish had to support orphans and those too old or ill to work, and lock up those thought fit but unwilling to work in 'bridewells' or 'houses of

*Beggars and vagrants were a cause of great concern (and not much compassion) in Shakespeare's day. They were whipped from parish to parish. Nobody wanted to bear the cost of keeping them.*

correction' until there was work for them to do. It charged householders a tax called the 'poor rate', to do this, but preferred to move people on. By law, a beggar could be whipped by the parish officers 'until his or her body be bloody', and sent back to his or her birthplace; but often it was simpler to send them on to the next parish to be whipped again. The Elizabethans assumed that most beggars were really swindlers, and as we shall see, some of them were.

The result was that almost any stranger (outside the teeming city of London) was regarded as suspicious. No wonder Shakespeare's Watch keep a careful eye on Conrade and Borachio. Among those the law classed as 'vagrants' and at risk of whipping were palmists, fencers, keepers of dancing bears, jugglers, pedlars and tinkers, plus some who

might seem more respectable. Scholars of Oxford and Cambridge could be whipped if they begged without their university's authority. Even travelling actors – perhaps performing Shakespeare's plays – were considered 'sturdy beggars', unless, like Shakespeare's company, they were legally the 'servants' of a rich patron.

## Thieves and swindlers

The underworld of Elizabethan England had its own slang, or 'cant', with words for different kinds of thieves and swindlers, the people they met and the things they did. Harman lists 23 different kinds of rogue, including 'Abraham men' (who pretended to be mad), 'dummerers' (who pretended to be dumb), 'hookers' (who stole clothes and linen from windows with a long, hooked pole), 'priggers of prancers' (horse-thieves) and 'upright men' (leading thieves who could take a share of any other thief's takings). Women were known as 'doxies', 'dells', or 'morts'; a rogue's wife was his 'autem (altar) mort'. Finding a fool and swindling him out of his money was called 'coney (rabbit) catching'.

London criminals came to the playhouses: to pick pockets, but also to see the plays. Some 'city comedies' featured underworld characters, and one, *The Roaring Girl*, by Thomas Middleton and Thomas Dekker, was about a real one. She was Marian Frith, or Moll Cutpurse, a prostitute and thief and a regular customer at the Fortune Theatre. She would sit on the stage with the court gallants, dressed in men's clothes (complete with a sword at her side) and smoking a pipe. She went to watch 'herself' – played by a boy, of course – in 1608. Shakespeare preferred to set most of his comedies in romantic foreign lands. But his underworld characters, and his parish officers, are rooted in the England of his time.

# The story of Much Ado About Nothing

Leonato, Governor of Messina, is in his orchard with his daughter Hero and niece Beatrice. He has a letter saying that his friend Don Pedro of Aragon is coming to Messina, after winning a great victory. One young man, Claudio, has been particularly brave.

Beatrice asks about another of Don Pedro's men – Signior Benedick, who visited Messina last year. Leonato explains that 'there is a kind of merry war' between Beatrice and Benedick: 'they never meet but there's a skirmish of wit between them'. A few moments later, Don Pedro and his companions arrive.

---

**Beatrice enquires of Benedick**

*He set up his bills here in Messina and challenged Cupid at the flight; and my uncle's fool, reading the challenge, subscribed for Cupid, and challenged him at the bird-bolt. I pray you, how many hath he killed and eaten in these wars? But how many hath he killed? For, indeed, I promised to eat all of his killing.*

*Who is his companion now? He hath every month a new sworn brother . . .*
*. . . he wears his faith but as the fashion of his hat; it ever changes with the next block.*

Act I Sc i

---

## Merry warriors

At once Beatrice and Benedick start their 'merry war' again. Leonato invites Don Pedro and his friends to stay. He makes a special point of welcoming Don John, Don Pedro's bastard brother. The brothers have quarrelled, but seem to have made peace. As Leonato leads his guests indoors, Claudio and Benedick linger outside to talk.

Claudio asks if Benedick has noticed Hero. Benedick dismisses her as dreary-looking. If only Beatrice were not 'possessed with a fury', she would be much more attractive. Benedick hopes his friend is not planning to 'thrust his neck into a yoke' by getting married.

---

**Benedick's vow**

*That a woman conceived me, I thank her; that she brought me up, I likewise give her most humble thanks: . . .*

*. . . Because I will not do them the wrong to mistrust any, I will do myself the right to trust none; and the fine is,– for the which I may go the finer,– I will live a bachelor.*

Act I Sc i

---

Don Pedro comes out to fetch his friends, and Benedick explains what they have been talking about. Don Pedro offers to help Claudio find out if Hero likes him. At a masked ball later in the evening, Don Pedro will talk to Hero and her father, pretending to be Claudio, and win her hand for his friend.

## False reports

Already, however, Don Pedro's plan is going awry. Leonato has been informed wrongly that rich Don Pedro means to woo Hero for himself.

While the others eat supper, the surly Don John talks to his friend Conrade. Despite their reconcilation Don John still resents his brother. Conrade tells him not to show his feelings, but he rejects this sensible advice.

Another friend of Don John's, Borachio, comes to tell him about Don Pedro's plan to woo Hero for Claudio. Don John, who is jealous of Claudio, wonders if he can use this news to cause trouble.

## Disguises and deception

After supper, Leonato waits for the masked revellers, gossiping with Antonio, Beatrice and Hero, and Hero's attendants Margaret and Ursula. Beatrice contrasts Don John's surly silence with Benedick's endless chatter, saying that the ideal man would be half-way between the two – as well as rich and good-looking. Leonato says his niece will never get a husband unless she curbs her sharp tongue. She says she thanks God every morning for not sending her one.

Don Pedro and his friends arrive, masked for the ball. Don Pedro leads Hero off to talk during the first dance; the other young men quickly choose partners. Benedick asks Beatrice, who pretends not to recognise him.

Don John, Borachio and Claudio are left without partners. The other two pretend to mistake Claudio for Benedick. Don John remarks that Don Pedro seems attracted to Hero, and asks Claudio to persuade him not to marry her, because she is not his equal.

Now Claudio is convinced that Don Pedro means to get Hero for himself. Benedick arrives and light-heartedly tells Claudio that he is a forsaken lover. Claudio takes it seriously and walks out.

**Claudio's mistrust**
*'Tis certain so; the prince woos for himself,*
*Friendship is constant in all other things*
*Save in the office and affairs of love:*
*Therefore all hearts in love use their own tongues;*
*Let every eye negotiate for itself*
*And trust no agent; for beauty is a witch*
*Against whose charms faith melteth into blood.*
*Farewell, therefore, Hero!*

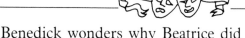

Act II Sc i

Benedick wonders why Beatrice did not recognise him. He decides to get his own back for her hard words. He sees Don Pedro coming with Hero and Leonato, and angrily speaks his mind about Beatrice.

**Benedick rages against Beatrice**
*She speaks poniards, and every word stabs: if her breath were*
*as terrible as her terminations, there were no living near her;*
*she would infect to the north star. I would not marry her,*
*though she were endowed with all that Adam had left him*
*before he transgressed:*

Act II Sc i

Now Beatrice and Claudio come in. Claudio, still upset, hardly speaks, but Beatrice makes up for him, saying his bad mood comes from jealousy. Don Pedro explains: Leonato has given permission for Claudio to marry Hero. Beatrice jokes about not having a husband, and Don Pedro offers to find her one. She leaves in a cheerful mood.

Don Pedro says Beatrice would make an excellent wife for Benedick. He offers to perform 'one of Hercules' labours': by the time Claudio and Hero are married, he will bring the warring couple together.

---

**Don Pedro's plot**

*I will teach you how to humour your cousin, that she shall fall in love with Benedick; and I, with your two helps, will so practise on Benedick that, in despite of his quick wit and his queasy stomach, he shall fall in love with Beatrice. If we can do this, Cupid is no longer an archer: his glory shall be ours, for we are the only love-gods.*

Act II Sc i

---

## Conspiracy

All looks bright for the future, but Don John is angry that his plan failed. Borachio suggests a new ploy to destroy Claudio's happiness. He will persuade Hero's maid, Margaret, to pretend to be Hero, saying good-bye to him as if he were her lover. Don John must bring Don Pedro and Claudio by to see this sight.

## Planting a seed

Benedick sits idly in Leonato's orchard, thinking about how Claudio has changed now that he is to be married. Once a plain-speaking soldier, who liked drum music and armour,

now he prefers dance music and fashionable clothes. It would take an extraordinary woman to have that effect on himself, he thinks.

**The woman for Benedick**
*Rich she shall be, that's certain; wise, or I'll none; virtuous, or I'll never cheapen her; fair, or I'll never look on her; mild, or come not near me; noble, or not I for an angel; of good discourse, an excellent musician, and her hair shall be of what colour it please God.*
Act II Sc iii

Don Pedro, Claudio, and Leonato slip into the orchard, bringing Balthazar to sing to them. They mean to let Benedick overhear their conversation. Balthazar's song should give him a clue: 'Men were deceivers ever'. Benedick's three friends talk about an astounding piece of news: Beatrice is in love with Benedick!

## The seed takes root

Benedick listens intently, at first in disbelief – this must be a joke – but gradually coming to think it is true. Don Pedro quietly asks Claudio to prepare Hero and Margaret for the next stage of his plan.

Beatrice comes in, to fetch Benedick in to dinner – against her will, she says. Though she speaks with her usual sharp tongue, Benedick now finds hidden meanings in her words – disguised messages of love.

## The women's plot

Now Hero, Ursula and Margaret set a trap for Beatrice. Margaret fetches her to hear Hero and Ursula talking about her. Hero says that Claudio has told her Benedick is in love with Beatrice; he and Don Pedro begged Hero to tell her about it, but she refused. Beatrice, she says, is too proud and self-centred to love anyone; if she knew Benedick loved her, she would only break his heart with teasing.

---

**Men have no chance**

> *I never yet saw man,*
> *How wise, how noble, young, how rarely featur'd,*
> *But she would spell him backward: if fair-fac'd,*
> *She would swear the gentleman should be her sister;*
> *If black, why, Nature, drawing of an antick,*
> *Made a foul blot; if tall, a lance ill-headed;*
> *If low, an agate very vilely cut;*
> *If speaking, why, a vane blown with all winds;*
> *If silent, why, a block moved with none.*
> *So turns she every man the wrong side out,*
>
> Act III Sc i

---

Beatrice, appalled at what she has heard about herself, decides to face Benedick.

> **Beatrice falls for the plot**
> *What fire is in mine ears? Can this be true?*
> *Stand I condemn'd for pride and scorn so much?*
> *Contempt, farewell! and maiden pride, adieu!*
> *No glory lives behind the back of such.*
> *And, Benedick, love on; I will requite thee,*
> *Taming my wild heart to thy loving hand.*
>
>
>
> Act III Sc i

### Benedick in love?

Don Pedro tells Claudio that as soon as the wedding is over, he must return to Aragon. Claudio offers to go with him, but Don Pedro refuses to take him from Hero so soon. Instead, Benedick must come – he is not in love and will be cheerful.

Claudio says maybe Benedick is in love – he is not as cheerful as he used to be. Benedick says he has toothache. Claudio points out that Benedick is being more careful about his appearance – he has even shaved off his beard. Don Pedro tries to take Claudio aside for a private word, but Don John interrupts them.

Setting his own malicious plan in motion, he asks Claudio to come with him tonight to Hero's chamber window. There he will see something that may make him change his mind about getting married.

### Messina's finest

As night falls, Master Constable Dogberry leads his men – the Watch – out to preserve law and order in Messina's streets. He takes his duties seriously, reminding the men of their job: to arrest vagrants, keep the streets quiet, send drunks home to bed and catch thieves. And they must watch Leonato's house, where a great crowd has gathered for Hero's wedding the next day.

Dogberry. *If you meet a thief, you may suspect him, by virtue of your office, to be no true man; and, for such kind of men, the less you meddle or make with them, why, the more is for your honesty.*

Second Watch. *If we know him to be a thief, shall we not lay hands on him?*

Dogberry. *Truly, by your office, you may; but I think they that touch pitch will be defiled. The most peaceable way for you, if you do take a thief, is, to let him show himself what he is and steal out of your company.*

Verges. *You have been always called a merciful man, partner.*

Act III Sc iii

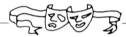

Dogberry and his deputy Verges leave the Watch to their task. At once they spot two obvious wrong-doers: Conrade and Borachio, whispering mysteriously about Don John's plan. Borachio has earned a thousand ducats by pretending to be 'Hero's' lover. Convinced by his act with Margaret at the window, Claudio has stormed off, swearing to shame Hero at the church by telling everyone what he saw.

The Watch find the story confusing, but they know villainy when they see it. 'In the Prince's name, stand!' cries one, arresting the pair. They lead them off, charging them with 'the most dangerous piece of lechery that was ever known in the commonwealth'.

## Wedding day

In the morning, Hero happily dresses for her wedding. Margaret helps her; she has no idea that what she did last night will hurt her mistress. Beatrice joins her cousin as she jokes about marriage with her two maids.

As Leonato is about to set off to church, Dogberry and Verges delay him by asking him to question their two

prisoners. Leonato tells them to do it themselves and they hurry off to the gaol. Leonato does not know that he has lost a chance to save his daughter's honour.

### Just cause?

Friar Francis takes Hero and Claudio through the marriage service. When Leonato 'gives' his daughter in marriage, Claudio asks what he can give in return, and offers Hero back to her father, abusively.

---

**Claudio rejects Hero**

*Give not this rotten orange to your friend;*
*She's but the sign and semblance of her honour.*
*Behold! how like a maid she blushes here.*
*O! what authority and show of truth*
*Can cunning sin cover itself withal.*

Act IV Sc i

---

All the congregation are shocked: Don Pedro is sorry he arranged for his friend to marry a 'common stale'. The men question Hero: she denies being unfaithful, but they do not believe her. Leonato calls for a dagger; in his shame, he wants to kill himself. Hero faints: only Beatrice and Benedick go to help her. Claudio, Don Pedro and Don John leave the church.

## Wronged innocence

Hero begins to revive. Leonato rages at her in self-pity; if she must shame him he would rather she were dead. Beatrice stands up for her cousin, but he will not listen. But now the

**Leonato abandons his daughter**

*. . . why, she–O! she is fallen*
*Into a pit of ink, that the wide sea*
*Hath drops too few to wash her clean again,*
*And salt too little which may season give*
*To her foul-tainted flesh.*

Act IV Sc i

Friar speaks up. He thinks Hero is innocent, and gently asks her who she is accused of meeting. She says she knows nothing about it. Benedick begins to suspect Don John's hand; Leonato threatens vengeance if his daughter has been falsely accused. The Friar suggests a plan to find out the truth: pretend Hero is dead, and see how Claudio reacts.

## A hard request

The Friar, Leonato and Hero leave Beatrice and Benedick alone. Beatrice is crying for her cousin's sake, and Benedick tries to console her. He admits that he loves her; what can he do for her? Her answer is simple: 'Kill Claudio!'

Benedick falters: is his friend now her enemy? Yes, says Beatrice, he has 'slandered, scorned, dishonoured my kinswoman'. If she were a man, she would kill him, but men today are too weak. Benedick overcomes his reluctance, and agrees to challenge Claudio to a duel.

## Justice

Meanwhile Dogberry laboriously questions Borachio and Conrade. Fortunately, a sensible church officer, the Sexton, prompts him to ask the watchmen what they heard the pair talking about. And so the plot is revealed; the Sexton points out that Hero *was* accused of unfaithfulness at the church, and that Don John has run away. He orders the prisoners to be taken to Leonato's.

## Vengeance

Leonato, who has come to believe Hero is innocent, challenges Claudio to fight. His brother Antonio offers to join in. Claudio refuses the challenge and Don Pedro tries to pacify the old men.

Now Benedick approaches Claudio and Don Pedro. Laughing, they tell him how they nearly had 'our two noses

---

**Beatrice challenges Benedick**

*O! that I were a man for his sake, or that I had any friend would be a man for my sake! But manhood is melted into curtsies, valour into compliment, and men are only turned into tongue, and trim ones too: he is now as valiant as Hercules, that only tells a lie and swears it. I cannot be a man with wishing, therefore I will die a woman with grieving.*

Act IV Sc i

snapped off with two old men without teeth'. But Benedick has a serious purpose: he too challenges Claudio. Gradually the others realise he is not joking.

### Claudio repents
Dogberry and the Watch come in with their prisoners, who confess the whole story. Claudio is horrified. Leonato and Antonio come in with the Sexton, who has told them the plot. Claudio offers to do any penance Leonato can name. Leonato orders him to make sure everyone knows Hero's name is clear, and to marry Antonio's daughter, his niece.

### Benedick the poet
Benedick is now definitely in love with Beatrice. He asks Margaret to bring her to talk to him. He has even been trying to write a poem about her, but has given up. When Beatrice comes, the two quickly admit they love each other. Ursula interrupts the lovers' conversation; Beatrice must go at once to her uncle's.

### An epitaph for Hero
*I cannot bid you bid my*
  *daughter live;*
*That were impossible: but, I*
  *pray you both,*
*Possess the people in Messina*
  *here*
*How innocent she died; and if*
  *your love*
*Can labour aught in sad*
  *invention,*
*Hang her an epitaph upon her*
  *tomb,*
*And sing it to her bones: sing it*
  *to-night.*

Act v Sc i

### Another wedding
As he promised, Claudio hangs an epitaph for Hero on Leonato's family tomb, and Balthazar sings a song of mourning for her. Now Claudio sets off to marry Leonato's niece.

She is waiting for him, masked, at Leonato's, with Friar Francis ready to marry them. Everyone is there, just as at the first ceremony. Claudio asks to see her face, but Leonato says he must make the marriage vows first. As Claudio does so, she removes her mask – it is Hero! Now Benedick asks to see Beatrice. She too removes her mask. He asks if she loves him; she pretends to take it lightly. Claudio and Hero produce papers – poems the other two have written to each other. They may deny it, but here is the proof in their own hands. At last, the warring couple kiss.

**Love and war**

Beatrice. *But for which of my good parts did you first suffer love for me?*

Benedick. *'Suffer love,' a good epithet! I do suffer love indeed, for I love thee against my will.*

Beatrice. *In spite of your heart, I think. Alas, poor heart! If you spite it for my sake, I will spite it for yours; for I will never love that which my friend hates.*

Benedick. *Thou and I are too wise to woo peaceably.*

Act v Sc ii

Since the Friar is here, they can get married immediately – but first, Benedick suggests, everyone must dance. Laughing, he tells Don Pedro to find a wife.

# The play's characters

Beatrice　　　　　　　　　　　Benedick

---

### Beatrice's tongue

*By my troth, niece, thou wilt never get thee a husband, if thou be so shrewd of thy tongue.*

Act II Sc ii

### Beatrice's daily prayer

*. . . if he send me no husband; for the which blessing I am at him upon my knees every morning and evening.*

Act II Sc ii

---

**Beatrice**
Beatrice is renowned as the brightest and wittiest of Shakespeare's women characters. Above all, she is independent. The men claim to be in fear of her sharp tongue, but when her cousin is deserted at the altar, she is the one who sees the truth and unconditionally takes Hero's side. Her great weakness is pride (Benedick greets her as 'my Lady Disdain'), and this is both what prevents her acknowledging that she loves Benedick from the start, and allows their friends to trick them into marriage at last. She cannot bear the idea that she is being condemned – even for her pride – and so determines to risk showing her feelings for once.

**Benedick**
Like Beatrice, Benedick is proud and perhaps over-concerned with his own 'image'. He likes to play the free-spirited man who will not be 'shackled' to a woman. But, again like Beatrice, he is kind and honourable under the witty mask. He is perhaps afraid of being hurt: once he has been fooled into thinking that Beatrice has owned her love for him, his attitude changes. At first, he lives up to Beatrice's description of him as a far from ideal husband: changeable, ridiculously over-dressed, and

egotistical, but as the play progresses we learn that he is a much more solid character. Once they stop quarrelling and showing off, it is obvious that the pair are well-suited.

### Hero

Hero shares her cousin's sense of humour and delight in life, but without the sharpness we see in Beatrice. She enjoys deceiving Benedick and Beatrice, but wants nothing but happiness for them and everyone else. She is so obviously charming and innocent that it is a shock when she is accused of unfaithfulness,

and even more so when others seem to believe the accusation. It is a great relief when Beatrice, Benedick and the Friar take her side.

### Claudio

Unlike the other main characters, Claudio lets his feelings rule over his good sense. One minute he is all charm and good fun, but once suspicion has entered his mind, he cannot even behave politely in church (or, indeed, ask Hero for her side of the story before they get to church). He can see Benedick's faults, but is blind to his own. But because he is

Leonato

charming and good-humoured at other times, and we know his sudden outbreaks of temper are rooted in real feelings, we (and Hero) forgive him.

### Leonato

Like many fathers in Shakespeare's plays, Leonato is fussy and concerned for his family. Unlike some others, he is unable to resist joining in the younger people's fun. When everything turns sour for Hero, he is devastated, but he has the good sense to take up the Friar's suggestion for bringing her and Claudio back together. This is an affectionate portrait of a pleasant, slightly comic man.

Hero

Claudio

Don John    Don Pedro

### Dogberry
This well-meaning, likeable official is one of Shakespeare's unwitting comics. He regularly misuses words and totally misunderstands the job of law enforcement. He advises his men to let all the wrongdoers go, and in the interests of their quiet good-behaviour, approves of them sleeping on duty.

### Don Pedro
The Prince of Aragon is an odd character, perhaps not all that different from his villainous brother. Both like to manipulate people and play games of deception. Why else should Don Pedro approach Hero and her father on Claudio's behalf in disguise? The difference is that Don Pedro sets up his complicated schemes to help others – even if sometimes he causes them problems at first – while Don John's motives are darker.

### Don John
Like Edmund in *King Lear*, Don John feels cheated by life and envious of his better-born brother. He resents his brother's forgiveness for their past quarrels, but he is dependent on him and so takes his anger out on Don Pedro's friends. He is one of many villains in Shakespeare who plot against others while presenting a friendly face to the world.

### Dogberry's kindness
*Truly, I would not hang a dog by my will, much more a man who hath any honesty in him.*
Act III Sc iii

Dogberry

### Don Pedro's good humour
*I was born to speak all mirth and no matter.*
Act II Sc iii

### Beatrice on Don John
*How tartly that gentleman looks! I never can see him but I am heart-burned an hour after.*
Act II Sc i

# The life and plays of Shakespeare

**Life of Shakespeare**

**1564** William Shakespeare born at Stratford-upon-Avon.

**1582** Shakespeare marries Anne Hathaway, eight years his senior.

**1583** Shakespeare's daughter, Susanna, is born.

**1585** The twins, Hamnet and Judith, are born.

**1587** Shakespeare goes to London.

**1591-2** Shakespeare writes *The Comedy of Errors*. He is becoming well-known as an actor and writer.

**1592** Theatres closed because of plague.

**1593-4** Shakespeare writes *Titus Andronicus* and *The Taming of the Shrew*: he is member of the theatrical company, the Chamberlain's Men.

**1594-5** Shakespeare writes *Romeo and Juliet*.

**1595** Shakespeare writes *A Midsummer Night's Dream*.

**1595-6** Shakespeare writes *Richard II*.

**1596** Shakespeare's son, Hamnet, dies. He writes *King John* and *The Merchant of Venice*.

**1597** Shakespeare buys New Place in Stratford.

**1597-8** Shakespeare writes *Henry IV*.

**1599** Shakespeare's theatre company opens the Globe Theatre.

**1599-1600** Shakespeare writes *As You Like It*, *Henry V* and *Twelfth Night*.

**1600-01** Shakespeare writes *Hamlet*.

**1602-03** Shakespeare writes *All's Well That Ends Well*.

**1603** Elizabeth I dies. James I becomes king. Theatres closed because of plague.

**1603-04** Shakespeare writes *Othello*.

**1605** Theatres closed because of plague.

**1605-06** Shakespeare writes *Macbeth* and *King Lear*.

**1606-07** Shakespeare writes *Antony and Cleopatra*.

**1607** Susanna Shakespeare marries Dr John Hall. Theatres closed because of plague.

**1608** Shakespeare's granddaughter, Elizabeth Hall, is born.

**1609** *Sonnets* published. Theatres closed because of plague.

**1610** Theatres closed because of plague. Shakespeare gives up his London lodgings and retires to Stratford.

**1611-12** Shakespeare writes *The Tempest*.

**1613** Globe Theatre burns to the ground during a performance of Henry VIII.

**1616** Shakespeare dies on 23 April.

**Shakespeare's plays**

The Comedy of Errors
Love's Labour's Lost
Henry VI Part 2
Henry VI Part 3
Henry VI Part 1
Richard III
Titus Andronicus
The Taming of the Shrew
The Two Gentlemen of Verona
Romeo and Juliet
Richard II
A Midsummer Night's Dream
King John
The Merchant of Venice
Henry IV Part 1
Henry IV Part 2
Much Ado About Nothing
Henry V
Julius Caesar
As You Like It
Twelfth Night
Hamlet
The Merry Wives of Windsor
Troilus and Cressida
All's Well That Ends Well
Othello
Measure for Measure
King Lear
Macbeth
Antony and Cleopatra
Timon of Athens
Coriolanus
Pericles
Cymbeline
The Winter's Tale
The Tempest
Henry VIII

# Index

Picture credits
p.1 Governors of Royal Shakespeare
Theatre, Stratford-upon-Avon, p.3 Ancient
Art and Architecture Collection, p.4/5 Scala,
p.7 Scala, p.8 Ancient Art and Architecture
Collection, p.10 Scala, p.11 The Kobal
Collection.